ALBERIC THE WISE

AND OTHER JOURNEYS

ALBERIC THE WISE
AND OTHER JOURNEYS

by

NORTON JUSTER

illustrated by
Domenico Gnoli

Alfred A. Knopf New York

THIS IS A BORZOI BOOK PUBLISHED BY ALFRED A. KNOPF

All rights reserved. Published in the United States by Alfred A. Knopf, an imprint of Random House Children's Books, a division of Random House, Inc., New York. Originally published in hardcover in the United States by Pantheon Books, a division of Random House, Inc., New York, in 1965.

Knopf, Borzoi Books, and the colophon are registered trademarks of Random House, Inc.

Visit us on the Web! www.randomhouse.com/kids

Educators and librarians, for a variety of teaching tools, visit us at www.randomhouse.com/teachers

The Library of Congress has cataloged the hardcover edition of this work as follows:
Juster, Norton.
Alberic the Wise, and other journeys / Norton Juster.
p. cm.
Contents: Alberic the Wise.—She cries no more.—Two kings.
PZ8.J98 Al
(OCoLC) 946373

ISBN 978-0-375-86699-9 (trade pbk.) — ISBN 978-0-375-96699-6 (lib. bdg.) —
ISBN 978-0-375-89730-6 (ebook)

Printed in the United States of America
November 2010
10 9 8 7 6 5 4 3 2 1

For my mother and father

Contents

Alberic the Wise
1

She Cries No More
27

Two Kings
61

More than many years ago when fewer things had happened in the world and there was less to know, there lived a young man named Alberic who knew nothing at all. Well, almost nothing, or depending on your generosity of spirit, hardly anything, for he could hitch an ox and plow a furrow straight or thatch a roof or hone his scythe until the edge was bright and sharp or tell by a sniff of the breeze what the day would bring or with a glance when a grape was sweet and ready. But these were only the things he had to know to live or couldn't help knowing by living and are, as you may have discovered, rarely accounted as knowledge.

Of the world and its problems, however, he knew little, and indeed was even less aware of their existence. In all his life he had been nowhere and seen nothing beyond the remote estate on which he lived and to whose lands he and his family had been bound back beyond the edge of memory. He planted and harvested, threshed and winnowed, tended the hives and the pigs, breathed the country air, and stopped now and again to listen to the birds or puzzle at the wind. There were no mysteries, hopes or dreams other than those that could be encompassed by his often aching back or impatient stomach. This was the sum of his existence and with it he was neither happy nor sad. He simply could not conceive of anything else.

Since the days were much alike he measured his life by the more discernible seasons—yet they too slipped easily by, and would have continued to do so, I'm sure, had it not been for the lone traveler who appeared unaccountably one chill morning at the close of winter. Alberic watched him make his weary way along the road until, when they stood no more

than a glance apart, he paused to rest before continuing on his journey. A curious old man— his tattered tunic was patched on patches and his worn shoes left hardly a suggestion of leather between himself and the cold ground. He carried a massive bundle on his back and sighed with the pleasure of letting it slide gently from his shoulder to the ground—then just as gently let himself down upon it. He nodded and smiled, mopped his face carefully with a handkerchief easily as old as himself, then acknowledged Alberic's timid greeting and finally began to speak, and when he did it was of many, many things. Where he had come from and where he was bound, what he had seen and what there was yet to discover—commonwealths, kingdoms, empires, counties and duke-doms—fortresses, bastions and great solitary castles that dug their fingers into the mountain passes and dared the world to pass—royal courts whose monarchs dressed in pheasant skins and silks and rich brocades of purple and lemon and crimson and bice all interlaced with figures of beasts and blossoms and strange geometric devices—and mountains that had no tops and oceans that had no bottoms.

There seemed no end to what he knew or what he cared to speak about, and speak he did, on and on through the day. His voice was soft and easy but his manner such that even his pauses commanded attention. And as he spoke his eyes sparkled and his words were like maps of unknown lands. He told of caravans that made their way across continents and back with perfumes and oils and dark red wines, sandalwood and lynx hides and ermine and carved sycamore chests, with

3

cloves and cinnamon, precious stones and iron pots and ebony and amber and objects of pure tooled gold—of tall cathedral spires and cities full of life and craft and industry—of ships that sailed in every sea, and of art and science and learned speculation hardly even dreamed of by most people—and of armies and battles and magic and much, much more.

Alberic stood entranced, trying desperately to imagine all these wonderful things, but his mind could wander no further than the fields that he could see and the images soon would fade or cloud.

4

"The world is full of wonders," he sighed forlornly, for he realized that he could not even imagine what a wonder was.

"It is everything I've said and even more," the stranger replied, and since it was by now late afternoon he scrambled to his feet and once more took up his heavy bundle. "And remember," he said with a sweep of his arm, "it is all out there, just waiting." Then down the road and across the stubble fields he went.

For weeks after the old man had gone Alberic brooded, for now he knew that there were things he didn't know, and what magic and exciting things they were! Warm wet breezes had begun to blow across the land and the frozen fields had yielded first to mud and then to early blossoms. But now this quiet hillside was not enough to hold his rushing thoughts. "It is all out there, just waiting," he said to himself again and again, repeating the old man's words. When he had repeated them often enough, they became a decision. He secretly packed his few belongings and in the early morning's mist left his home and started down into the world to seek its wonders and its wisdom.

For two days and nights and half another day again he walked—through lonely forests and down along the rushing mountain streams that seemed to know their destination far better than he knew his. Mile after mile he walked until at last the trees and vines gave way to sweeps of easy meadowland and in the distance, barely visible, the towers of a city reflected back the sun's bright rays. As he approached, the hazy form became a jumble of roofs and chimney pots spread out below, and each step closer embellished them with windows, carved gables, domes and graceful spires. All this in turn was circled by a high wall which seemed to grow higher and wider as he descended towards it until at last it filled his vision and hid all else behind it. The stream which only days before had been so gay and playful now broadened and as if aware of its new importance assumed a slow and dignified pace as it passed through the city. Alberic paused for a moment to catch his breath, then, with a slight shiver of anticipation, passed beneath the cool dark gates and entered the city too.

What a teeming, busy place! Houses and shops, music and movement, all kinds of noises, signs and smells, and more people than he ever knew existed. He wandered along the cobbled streets delighted by each new discovery and noting with care the strange new sights and sounds so unfamiliar to his country senses. He soon learned too that he had come to a city famous above all others for the beautiful stained glass manufactured in its workshops.

"A noble and important profession," he decided soberly, "for surely beauty is the true aim of wisdom!" Without delay he went off to apprentice himself to the greatest of the master glassmakers.

"Well, well," growled the old craftsman after examining Alberic carefully, "so you want to make glass. Very well, we shall see. Your duties will be few and simple. Each morning you'll rise before the birds and with the other apprentices fetch sixty barrows of firewood from the forest. Then in each furnace bank a fire precisely hot enough to melt the lead and fuse the glass, and keep them tended constantly so that none goes out or varies even slightly in its heat. Then, of course, work the bellows, fetch the ingots from the foundry, run errands, assist the journeymen as they need, sharpen and repair all the chisels, files, knives, scrapers, shears, mallets and grozing irons so that each is in perfect order, make deliveries quickly and courteously, grind and mix the pigments, work the forge, sweep out the shop, fetch, carry, stoop, haul and bend, and in your spare time help with the household chores. You can of course eat your fill of the table scraps and sleep on the nice warm floor. Well, don't just stand there, you've only started and you're already hours behind in your work." When he finished he smiled a benevolent smile, for he was known for his generous nature.

Alberic applied himself to his new tasks with diligence,

working from early morning until late at night when he would curl up in one corner of the shop to dream happily of the day's accomplishments and carefully sort and pack into his memory everything he'd learned. For some time he did only the menial jobs, but soon under the watchful eye of the master he began taking part in more important and exacting procedures. He learned to chip and shape the glass into pieces often no larger than the palm of his hand and then apply the colors mixed in gum or oil with a delicate badger brush and fire these to permanence in the glowing kilns. Then from measurements and patterns he learned to set each piece in the grooved strips of lead and solder them carefully at each joint. For almost two years he worked and watched as all these small and painstaking operations took form in great windows and medallions of saintly lives or tales of moral instruction which glowed in deep splendid blues and vivid rubies.

Finally the time came for Alberic to prove his skill and take his place among the glassmakers—to create a work entirely on his own. He was determined that it would be a rare and lovely thing and he set about it with quiet intensity.

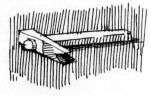

"What will it be, Alberic?" they all asked eagerly.

"Beautiful," he replied with never a moment's doubt, and that was all he'd say.

And for weeks he worked secretly in one corner of the shop until the day came when his work was to be judged. Everyone gathered to see it. The master looked long and carefully. He stood back to view it in the light and squinted close at matters of fine detail, and then he rubbed his chin and then he tapped his finger and then he swayed and then he sighed and then he frowned.

"No," he said sadly and slowly, "certainly not. You will never be a glassmaker." And everyone agreed, for despite the best of intentions Alberic's work was poor indeed.

How miserable he was! How thoroughly miserable! Why wasn't it beautiful when he had tried so hard? How could he have learned so much and yet still fail? No one knew the answer. "There is no reason now for me to stay," he said quietly, gathering up his bundle, and without even as much as a last look back he walked out into the lonely countryside. For several days he wandered aimlessly, seeing nothing, heading nowhere, his thoughts turned inward to his unhappy failure.

But it was spring and no one who has ever worked the land can long ignore the signs this season brings. Sweet promising smells hung gently in the warm air, and all around the oxlips, daisies and celandine splashed the fields in lively yellow. A graceful bird and then another caught Alberic's eye. The busy buzz and click of smaller things were reassuring to his ear and even the bullfrogs' heavy thump set his heart beating once again. His spirits and then his hope revived. The world seemed large and inviting once again.

"There are other places and other things to learn," he thought. "Beauty isn't everything. The true measure of wisdom is utility. I'll do something useful." He hurried now and before long came to a city whose stonecutters and masons were renowned throughout the world for the excellence of their work. His thoughts turned to castles and cloisters, massive walls, towering vaults and steeples which only miracles of skill could hold suspended in the air.

"Everything of use and value is made of stone," he concluded, and rushed to seek employment with the master stonecutter.

And for two more years he busied himself learning the secrets of this new vocation—selecting and cutting only the finest stone from the quarry—matching, marking and extracting the giant blocks to be moved on heavy wheeled carts to each new building—and then noting carefully how each shaped stone was fitted in its place so that walls and buttresses grew and arches sprang from pier to pier with such precision that no blade however sharp could slip between the joints. Soon he learned to mix and measure mortar and operate the windlasses whose ingenious ropes and pulleys allowed one man to lift for fifty. Then to make his first careful cuts with bolster and chisel and then stop and watch again as surer hands than his cut and shaped the graceful moldings and intricate tracery which brought the stone to life. As he worked he questioned and remembered everything he saw and heard, and as each day passed, his confidence and his knowledge grew and he began to think of his future life as a great and skillful stonecutter.

When the time came for him to prove his skill to the masons and sculptors of the guild, Alberic chose a piece of specially fine, delicately veined marble and set to work. It was to be the finest carving they had ever seen. With great care he studied and restudied the block and planned his form, then cut into the stone in search of it. He worked in a fever of excitement, his sharp chisels biting off the unwanted material in large chips and pieces. But the image he saw so clearly in his mind seemed always to be just out of sight, a little deeper in the stone. The block grew smaller and the mound of dust and chips larger, and still, like a phantom, the form seemed to recede and still he chased it. Soon there was nothing left at all. The great block of stone had disappeared and soon after, the stonecutter too. For again, without a word, Alberic gathered up his belongings and passed through the city gate. He had failed once more.

"Usefulness isn't everything," he decided after roaming about disconsolately for several days. "Innovation is surely a measure of wisdom. I'll do something original."

The opportunity presented itself in the very next town, where the goldsmiths, it was said, produced objects of unsurpassed excellence and fancy. Bowls and magic boxes, mirrors, shields and scepters, crowns, rings, enchanted buckles and clasps, and candlesticks and vases of incredible grace and intricacy spilled from these workshops and found their way to every royal court and market in the land. It was here that Alberic learned to draw and shape the fine gold wire and work the thin sheets of metal into patterns and textures of light and shape and then inlay these with delicate enamels and precious stones. It was here also that he worked and hoped for the next two years of his life and it was here that for the third time he failed and for the third time took his disappointment to the lonely countryside.

And so it went, from town to town, from city to city, each noted for its own particular craft or enterprise. There were potters who turned and shaped their wet clay into graceful bowls and tall jugs fire-glazed with brilliant cobalt, manganese and copper oxides. Leather finishers who transformed smooth soft skins into shoes and boots, gloves, tunics, bombards, bottles and buckets. There were weavers and spinners who worked in wools and silks, carpenters and cabinetmakers, glassblowers,

armorers and tinkers. There were scholars who spent their days searching out the secrets of ancient books, and chemists and physicians, and astronomers determining the precise distances between places that no one had ever seen. And busy ports which offered men the sea and all it touched, and smiths and scribes and makers of fine musical instruments, for anyone with such a bent. Alberic tried them all—and watched and learned and practiced and failed and then moved on again. Yet he kept searching and searching for the one thing that he could do. The secret of the wisdom and skill he so desired.

The years passed and still he traveled on—along the roads and trails and half-forgotten paths—across plains and deserts and forests whose tangled growth held terrors that were sometimes real and sometimes even worse—over hills and cruel high mountain passes and down again perhaps along some unnamed sea—until at last, alone and old and tired, he reached the ramparts of the great capital city.

"I will never find wisdom," he sighed. "I'm a failure at everything."

At the edge of the market square Alberic set his bundle down and watched longingly as all the students, artisans and craftsmen went unconcernedly about their business. He wiped the dust from his eyes and sat for a moment, thinking of his future and his past. What a strange sight he was! His beard was now quite long and grey and the cloak and hat and shoes bore evidence of some repair from every place he'd been. His great bundle bulged with the debris of a lifetime's memories and disappointments and his face was a sad scramble of much the same. As he rummaged through his thoughts, a group of children, struck by his uncommon look, stopped and gathered close around him.

"Where have you come from?"

"What do you do?"

"Tell us what you've seen," they eagerly asked, and poised to listen or flee as his response required.

Alberic was puzzled. What could he tell them? No one had ever sought his conversation before, or asked his opinion on any question. He scratched his head and rubbed his knees, then slowly and hesitantly began to speak, and suddenly the sum of all those experiences, which lay packed up in his mind as in some disordered cupboard, came back to him. He told them of a place or two he'd been and of some lands they'd never known existed and creatures that all their wildest fancies could not invent, and then a story, a legend and three dark mysterious tales remembered from a

thousand years before. As he spoke, the words began to come more easily and the pleasure of them eased away his weariness. Everything he'd ever seen or heard or touched or tried was suddenly fresh and clear in his memory, and when the children finally left for home, their faces glowing with excitement, it was to spread the news of the wonderful old man who knew so much.

Since he had no place else to go, Alberic returned to the square each day, and each day the crowds grew larger and larger around him. At first it was only the children, but soon everyone, regardless of age or size, crowded close to listen— and patiently he tried to tell them all they wished to hear. For many of their questions his own experience provided the answers, and for those he could not directly answer he always had a tale or story whose point or artifice led them to answers of their own. More and more he began to enjoy the days and soon he learned to embellish his tales with skillful detail, to pause at just the right time, to raise his voice to a roar or lower it to a whisper as the telling demanded. And the crowds grew even larger.

Workmen came to listen and stayed to learn the secret ways and methods of their own crafts. Artisans consulted him on questions of taste or skill and when they left they always knew more than when they came. Alberic told them everything he had learned or seen through all his failures and his wanderings, and before very long he became known throughout the realm as Alberic the Wise.

His fame spread so far that one day the King himself and several of his ministers came to the square to see for themselves. Cleverly disguised so as not to alert the old man to his purpose, the King posed several questions concerning matters of state and situations in far-off corners of the kingdom. Everything he asked, Alberic answered in great detail, enlarging each reply with accounts of the lore and customs of each region, condition of the crops and royal castles, local problems and controversies, reports on

the annual rainfall and the latest depredations by various discontented barons. And for added measure, two songs and a short play (in which he acted all the parts) which he had learned before being dismissed from a traveling theater company.

"You are the wisest man in my kingdom," the astonished King proclaimed, throwing off his disguise, "and you shall have a palace of your own with servants and riches as befits a man of your accomplishments."

Alberic moved into the new palace at once and was more than content with his new life. He enjoyed the wealth and possessions he had never known before, slept on feather beds, ate nothing but the most succulent and delicate foods and endlessly put on and took off the many cloaks, robes and caps the King had graciously provided. His beard was trimmed and curled and he spent his time strolling about the gardens and marble halls posing with proper dignity before each mirror and repeating to himself in various tones and accents, "Alberic the Wise, ALBERIC THE WISE, A-L-B-E-R-I-C T-H-E W-I-S-E!" in order to become accustomed to his new title.

After several weeks, however, the novelty began to wear thin, for a sable cloak is just a sable cloak and a *poulet poêle à l'estragon* is really just another roast chicken. Soon doubts began to crowd out pleasures and by degrees he grew

first serious, then sober, then somber and then once again thoroughly discouraged.

"How is it possible to be a failure at everything one day and a wise man the next?" he inquired. "Am I not the same person?"

For weeks this question continued to trouble him deeply, and since he could not find a satisfactory answer he returned to the square with his doubts.

"Simply calling someone wise does not make him wise!" he announced to the eager crowd. "So you see, I am not wise." Then, feeling much better, he returned to the palace and began to make ready to leave.

"How modest," the crowd murmured. "The sign of a truly great man." And a delegation of prominent citizens was sent to prevail on him to stay.

Even after listening to their arguments Alberic continued to be troubled and the very next day he returned to the square again.

"Miscellaneous collections of fact and information are not wisdom," he declared fervently. "Therefore I am not wise!" And he returned and ordered workmen to begin boarding up the palace.

"Only the wisest of men would understand this," the people all agreed, and petitions were circulated to prevent his leaving.

For several more days he paced the palace corridors unhappily and then returned for a third time.

"A wise man's words are rarely questioned," he counseled gently. "Therefore you must be very careful whom you call wise."

The crowd was so grateful for his timely warning that they cheered for fully fifteen minutes after he had returned to the palace.

Finally, in desperation, he reappeared that very afternoon and stated simply, "For all the years of my life I have sought wisdom and to this day I still do not know even the meaning of the word, or where to find it," and thinking that would convince them he ordered a carriage for six o'clock that afternoon.

The crowd gasped. "No one but a man of the most profound wisdom would ever dare to admit such a thing," they all agreed, and an epic poem was commissioned in his honor.

Once again Alberic returned to the palace. The carriage was canceled, the rooms were opened and aired. There was nothing he could say or do to convince them that he wasn't what they all thought him to be. Soon he refused to answer any more questions or, in fact, to speak at all and everyone agreed that because of the troubled times this was certainly the wisest thing to do. Each day he grew more morose and miserable, and though his fame continued to grow and spread he found no more satisfaction in his success than he had in all his failures. He slept little and ate less and his magnificent robes began to hang like shrouds. The bright optimism that had shone in his eyes through all his travels and hardships began to fade and as the months passed he took to spending all his time at the top of the great north tower, staring without any interest at nothing in particular.

"I am no wiser now than I was before," he said one afternoon, thinking back across the years. "For I still don't know what I am or what I'm looking for." But as he sat there remembering and regretting, he sensed in the air the barest suggestion of some subtle yet familiar scent that drifted in on the freshening breeze. What it was he didn't know—perhaps the pungent tangled aroma of some far eastern bazaar or the sharp and honest smell of a once-known workshop, or it might have been simply the sweet clean air of an upland field the memory of which had long been lost in detail yet retained in some more durable way; but whatever it was it grew stronger and stronger, stirring something deep within him and taking hold of all his thoughts and feelings. His spirit suddenly quickened in response and each breath now came faster than the one before.

And then for just a moment he sat quite still—and then at last he knew.

"I am not a glassmaker nor a stonecutter, nor a goldsmith, potter, weaver, tinker, scribe or chef," he shouted happily, and he leaped up and bounded down the steep stone stairs. "Nor a vintner, carpenter, physician, armorer, astronomer, baker or boatman." Down and around he ran as fast as he could go, along the palace corridors until he reached the room in which all his old things had been stored. "Nor a blacksmith, merchant, musician or cabinetmaker," he continued as he put on the ragged cloak and shoes and hat. "Nor a wise man or a fool, success or failure, for no one but myself can tell me what I am or what I'm not." And when he'd finished he looked into the mirror and smiled and wondered why it had taken him so long to discover such a simple thing.

So Alberic picked up his bundle, took one last look through the palace and went down to the square for the last time.

"I have at last discovered one thing," he stated simply. "It is much better to look for what I may never find than to find what I do not really want." And with that he said goodbye and left the city as quietly as he'd come.

The crowd gasped and shook their heads in disbelief.

"He has given up his palace!"

"And his wealth and servants!"

"And the King's favor!"

"And he does not even know where he is going," they buzzed and mumbled. "How fool-ish, how very foolish! How could we ever have thought him wise?" And they all went home.

But Alberic didn't care at all, for now his thoughts were full of all the things he had yet to see and do and all the times he would stop to tell his stories and then move on again. Soon the walls were far behind and only his footsteps and the night were there to keep him company. Once again he felt the freedom and the joy of not knowing where each new step would take him, and as he walked along his stride was longer and stronger than was right somehow for a man his age.

His name was Claude, but it could have been Gerald or Malcolm or Arnold or Harold or Samuel. It made no difference to him at all—hardly anything did. If something was or it wasn't, if it happened or it didn't, were it hispid or glabrous, it was all the same to Claude, for he had decided at his last birthday that there was no way to be absolutely sure of anything. There were always two sides to every question and for every yes a no (not counting all the maybes). What one person liked another despised. What someone thought was surely right another was bound to find as surely wrong. And then besides all that, everything was always changing anyway. As soon as you'd become accustomed to summer, it became winter, afternoons invariably turned to evenings, the sixth grade to the seventh and friendships to only memories. Every time he thought about it he became more convinced that there was nothing that was really true and even less in which to believe. So it was simpler not to care about anything, for in that way he was never disappointed.

"It doesn't matter," he'd often say, or, "It's not my concern," or, "I couldn't care less," or simply, "So what?"

It was difficult, however, to determine all this just by looking at him. At first glance, in fact, he was not too different from any other twelve-year-old boy—smaller than most perhaps, but still bigger than some. His hair was long and dark, his eyes quiet and almost brown (they were almost green and almost blue also, depending on the light and the color of his necktie). His nose, with only the slightest hesitation, pointed generally in the direction he was going and his mouth, since he rarely either smiled or frowned, held a neutral ground between the two. You could almost say he was handsome, if you didn't say it loud enough for him to hear you.

Of course, if you happened to be looking at him when he was shuffling through the snow with his hands buried deep in the pockets of his shaggy overcoat, his collar up, his cap down and a long scarf wrapped around what was left, it would have been difficult to tell anything at all—except, perhaps, that his shoes were wet and, if he was moving a little faster than usual, that he was most probably on his way to the museum.

Now if it *could* be said that Claude enjoyed anything, it was his visits to the museum. At least there the pictures never changed. From one day to the next you could be sure they would remain exactly the same, and then too the skies were bluer than real blue skies, the trees fuller, the victories more heroic, and the flowers never died. So those afternoons on which there was little else to do found him wandering through the quiet halls and galleries—on a ship that always sailed a brilliant sea, in a parade that went on and on forever, as an emperor whose word was always law, or at a banquet where the good things never ran out—and even knowing, as we all do, that such things are impossible, he did, on occasion, forget, and often it was only the closing bell echoing off the great rotunda ceiling which reminded him that, for better or worse, he was here and not there.

Before long Claude had come to know each and every painting in the collection, or so he thought, for late one day as he was returning from the exhibition of Spanish masters he saw one that he had never noticed before—hanging in the little alcove behind the marble stair which led to the collection of bronzes, faïence, terra cottas, enamels, ivory and wood carvings, plaquettes, medals, coins and wax reliefs on the second and third floors.

It was a small painting in a modest frame, carved and gilded. A plaque identified it simply as "A Young Lady in a Make-Believe Landscape," and while it could not be said with certainty who the artist had been, it was thought most probably to have been painted in the late fifteenth century by someone of the Florentine school.

The young lady stood in the center foreground of the picture. (Although it seemed odd to call her a lady, for she looked scarcely older than he.) Her right hand held a flower and rested gracefully on the edge of a table, the kind that appears so often at the corner or bottom of a painting so that ladies will have a place on which to rest their hands gracefully. Her dress was red, cut low and straight and laced down the front in the fashion of the day. Her hair parted in the middle with most of it pulled back into a little white cap, while the rest hung in loose curls at the sides. She was fair and pale with only the faintest touch of color in her cheeks and she was very beautiful. From her left a road entered the picture, disappeared behind her, then reappeared at her right shoulder, curved, dipped and appeared again at the left before turning to follow a slow silver river back into the landscape. Whether the landscape was real or make-believe he couldn't say, for to him it was no more real or make-believe than the lady herself, but there were hills and paths, an arched bridge across the river, a few boats, some pine and poplar, a manor wall and garden some distance away, a castle not quite seen in the background and a suggestion of much more just out of sight in the distant haze.

It was pleasant enough, he thought, though hardly worth a great deal of his time. Nevertheless, there was *something* in it that held him. Perhaps it was the composition, or the quality of the line, or the delicate use of color, or even the lady's eyes. Yes, most probably her eyes, for they were so very sad—and it was the kind of sadness that expected nothing ever to change. Yet with that they seemed also, in some way, to be searching and questioning and what was most disturbing was that the longer he stood there, the more they seemed to be questioning him.

"She's a sad one all right," said a guard who had paused for a moment behind him in the dimly lit alcove. "Hardly ever has a visitor. I expect she's lonely." He smiled at his little joke and then moved on again to the other side of the hall.

"Sad indeed," Claude mumbled, for he didn't like to be told what he had already seen for himself. "What does it

matter anyway?" He turned and headed for the large glass doors in the lobby. It was late and so he pushed quickly out into the street without giving it another thought—but then how could he have known what was to happen?

On his next visit he spent most of his time in the south wing with the seventeenth- and eighteenth-century French paintings and it was late afternoon again when he suddenly remembered the Young Lady. Without knowing why, he returned to look at her once more before leaving.

During the following weeks he found his thoughts returning constantly to the little painting, no matter where he was in the museum or what he had come to see, and for some unaccountable reason felt compelled to spend a part of each visit with it. Why? It was not the most beautiful painting there, nor the most interesting nor the most famous, and they couldn't have thought much of it themselves, hanging it in that dark, out-of-the-way place.

"I really don't care one way or the other," he found it necessary to tell himself repeatedly. Yet there he stood, studying it, examining it, trying to understand the reason for each brushstroke and marveling at the skill with which the artist could suggest a leaf or a bit of silk or the warmth and softness of her cheek with no more than paint on canvas. Soon he knew every jagged edge of every improbable rock, the number of silver links that shone in her necklace and even the time it would take to walk from where he stood to the farthest hill. Each time Claude returned he found himself drawn more closely to it and at times it even felt as if the soft warm light which filled the picture extended beyond the edges of the frame to fill the alcove around him. And then, what of her? Who was she? And what caused her such grief? For despite his determination to remain unconcerned, these were questions that troubled him.

"How would I ever find out, though?" he asked himself finally. "And why should I bother? It's silly and so is the museum." And so from that afternoon when he left he didn't return for almost a month.

When he did, it was to the alcove that he went first. Perhaps she was no longer there? But of course nothing had changed. Everything was exactly as it had been—well, almost everything, for just as he was about to leave again his attention was drawn to something on the floor directly below the painting. It was a small clear pool of liquid. Now that was curious. He looked from the pool to the painting and from the painting back to the pool—but how foolish! What could the painting have had to do with it?

"I didn't know she would miss me enough to cry," he said, pretending to be quite serious, and he laughed, but right in the middle he stopped, for the idea suddenly did not seem too far-fetched. After all, in a way he had missed her too.

"That's ridiculous," he insisted, and now he was impatient with himself for considering such nonsense. "There are a hundred explanations and that's the least likely. Anyway it will be gone tomorrow."

But it wasn't, for he returned to make certain, and this time the pool of water was ever so slightly larger. Now he was not sure what was ridiculous. He stepped closer to examine the painting carefully, looking for  some clue or sign or perhaps even the beginning of a tear. How quiet the museum was that afternoon—more quiet than he had ever remembered—and the air seemed warm to him, sweet and summery. Another step, still nothing, and another, still closer, leaning forward until he was no more than a few inches from the painting and still he could see nothing. There was now a clear smell of pine in the air and with it the vaguest hint of a delicate perfume. A rustling sound, like a gentle gust of wind through leaves, broke the silence and something very like a strand of long blond hair brushed his face.

Claude suddenly became quite dizzy, and reached back for support, but instead of the marble banister he found himself clutching a gnarled and twisted tree trunk. He gasped

and pulled his hand away as if it had touched a hot iron—then he jumped back, for now he noticed that instead of the marble floor there was grass under his feet. He held his breath—and he could feel the shiny surface of the painting pressing against his back.

"You mustn't be startled," she said quietly. "It's only an olive tree. They are really quite beautiful this time of year."

So it had happened at last! He was not *really* surprised, he told himself. It was just that it had happened at that very moment and in that way. He pressed his fingertips together to make sure that he was really there, or somewhere, and then he let his breath out slowly. For several moments they stood looking at each other.

"How thoughtless of me, though," she continued. "You must be dreadfully warm in that heavy coat. Please, come with me." She took his hand and led him around a grass bank and through a grove of trees just out of sight to the left. As they walked further on, her likeness remained in the foreground of the painting, as it had been, for she took with her all that was really herself, and left behind only the artist's recollection, for anyone who should happen along.

"No, no one will miss us," she assured him, anticipating

36

his thoughts. "They will not know I am gone, and will certainly never believe that you are here."

They found a pleasant place to sit on a low stone wall that stretched across and around a small field and they talked, and what was unusual was that they did so not as two people who had just met, but as if they were old friends.

"But Claudio is a lovely name," she insisted. How much nicer it sounded the way she said it. "And you must call me Elena."

Her voice was as clear and soft as he would have expected and if she didn't look as unhappy as he had thought she was, she was even more beautiful. There didn't seem to be any opportunity for all the questions Claude had meant to ask. Indeed, they slipped his mind entirely as he and Elena spent the afternoon earnestly discussing the shapes of the clouds, the reasons for names, the places they had never been and how far a bird could fly and still come home again—and they would probably have gone right on doing so had it not been for the bell which sounded far in the distance, as if from another world.

"Oh dear, it is the museum bell," Elena said, jumping to her feet. "It's six o'clock and you must leave now." They walked quickly back to the edge of the picture. Now Claude suddenly remembered that he still did not know how he had gotten there or why, or for that matter very much more than

37

he had known before. "I do hope you can come again," she said, touching his arm lightly, and before he could say anything he felt the air around him thicken and the cold marble floor beneath his shoes. And there in the painting Elena looked out at him sadly, just as before.

Claude spent a restless night. Did it really happen? Could it have happened? Should he go back? "I'm sure I shouldn't," he mumbled before dropping off to sleep, and for one full day he didn't. On the following afternoon, however, he did return to the museum. There on the floor was a fresh pool of water, or if you prefer now, tears, and almost before he could decide whether or not he wanted to go—he'd gone.

"Good afternoon," Elena said gravely. "I was afraid you wouldn't return, and it's such a lovely day for a picnic." If he had entered the picture or if it had simply reached out and engulfed him he wasn't sure, but he did know that he was there because she wanted him to be, and in another minute they had already started down the road—walking for a while along the river near the jujube trees, then across the bridge and up an easy slope along the opposite bank. As they walked, Elena told him many things about the valley and all that they could see from where they stood and even much that lay beyond. Before the afternoon had ended he'd learned the names and uses of all the native herbs and plants, the styles of architecture, the great works of the artists and scholars, and the size and aspect of the neighboring cities and kingdoms. He learned too that the manor house with its handsome courts and gardens had been built by her great-great-great-granduncle Ludovico the Tempestuous shortly after he had acquired the land more than two hundred years before—and that since then the valley had been ruled by her family. Yes, all these things he had learned, but not a thing more about Elena herself.

During the next week, Claude returned every afternoon and each time the tears were there to let him know how long he'd been away, and so too was Elena. She was so good and kind and soon he found he not only loved the days but her as

39

well, and had almost forgotten not to care. They wandered happily through the fields and vineyards, the small quiet farms and on occasion the ruins of the old castle itself, and it was only at those odd moments when she did not think he was looking that the care and sadness would return momentarily to her face. Yet when he asked, she would smile sweetly and show him the oldest tree that grew in the valley or the grotto where a wise man once lived.

One day, though, while Elena was busily chasing a butterfly, Claude started up the hill that somehow they had always managed to avoid. For several days he'd felt certain that sounds, vague yet persistent, were coming from the other side—rumbling and clanking and what he thought to be muffled shouts and voices—but each time, he was told it was only the wind. When he had almost reached the top Elena looked up and noticed for the first time where he was going.

"Stop, come down!" she shouted, but too late, for in three more steps he had reached the top.

There below and before him stretched another part of the valley and a great battle raging within it. *Confusion! Chaos! Turmoil! Desolation! Destruction!* Horsemen galloped and wheeled and galloped again across the blackened ground, clouds of dust mingled with the choking smoke of cannon. Infantry with pikes and crossbows charged across the field and fell. Wagons raced back and

forth and monstrous siege engines were being pushed slowly towards the walls of the city, which was fiercely resisting the attack—a city which for some reason had never been mentioned in their conversations.

"Come away," said Elena when she had reached his side, and her eyes now showed all the unhappiness that he had seen on the first day he'd found her.

"But why have you never told me?" Claude asked quietly.

"Please come away," she repeated. "It is not your concern."

As she spoke, below and to the left a fresh assault on the city had begun. The mangonels hurled their great stones against the thick walls until they had opened a small breach next to one of the towers. Hundreds of foot soldiers charged towards it across the open ground, but before they had gone even halfway the crossbows from the wall had begun to play their deadly music and the whine of arrows filled the air. Most of the attackers fell where they were hit. The few who

were unlucky enough to reach the walls were dispatched in ways less quick and merciful, and even before the dust had settled, repairs had begun and the breach was closed.

"What is the reason?" Claude asked again, stunned by the sight of such pain and horror. "Who is fighting and why?"

Before Elena could answer, the museum bell once again announced the end of the day. "Tomorrow," she promised hastily. How thankful for the delay she seemed.

The next day Elena did her best to direct Claude's attention elsewhere, suggesting among other things a visit to the nearby monastery, well known for its good works and even more renowned for the excellence of its chapel—the finest example of its particular style in the region. But he would not be turned away, and back up and over the hill they went. The battle still raged. It was terrible, and yet to Claude it was in a way also fascinating and unreal, seeing all those distant figures moving about like the pieces in a game. He moved forward, down the hill, closer, leading Elena by the hand. When they had reached the shelter of a large boulder only a few hundred yards away they stopped, and with no other delay possible she reluctantly told her story.

"This valley had always been so peaceful," she began, "and even though things at times were less than perfect, the farms were good, the city busy and prosperous and our situation far removed from the routes of invasion and plunder

that brought desolation to so much of the country. My father was Duke Grifonetto, the fourteenth of his line, and he was a just and good ruler. During his reign the main piazza was paved, three new wells were dug, the south gate was repaired and refaced with the finest marbles carved and decorated in classical motifs, the library was established and grain storehouses built to ensure supplies of food in the event of unforeseen hardships. Life was so happy in the palace." She sighed, touching her handkerchief lightly to the corner of her eye before going on. "But there were some among us who were not satisfied." And her mood darkened suddenly. "Led by the disaffected son of one of our own noble houses, an evil young man named Buto, they plotted to destroy the government and take everything for themselves. First they gained entry to the palace and my father's service. Then, in his name and without his knowledge, they raised the taxes, using the money for their own purposes, and sold the food in the warehouses for their own gain also. Rumors concerning my father's honesty were spread and soon they hardened into lies. Old friends turned against us and all confidence in the ruling family was destroyed. Merchants were forced to pay tribute or flee and when my father discovered all this it was too late, for Buto and his brigands had gained control of the army and the arsenal. Soon all justice vanished and the rights of the citizens were taken away. No longer could anyone speak his mind or sell his merchandise in freedom, and even thinking became a hazardous occupation. The weak were plundered and for those who resisted there was only death—or worse. My family and I were cast into the filthy dungeon beneath the old citadel, and the city fell into the hands of this fearsome tyrant and his mercenary soldiers."

Claude listened intently, his anger rising at her account of such villainy and injustice. For the better part of the afternoon she continued the story, telling him in greater detail of the plots and intrigues that caused her father's downfall—the burning of the courts of law, the strange disappearance of three chests from the city treasury, the spoiling of the city's water supply—and as she spoke, the constant sound of swords and fighting men could be heard in the background.

"But what then?" Claude asked eagerly. "Where is your family and how did this battle begin?"

"There were some who remained loyal," she continued. Now they had crept even

closer to the battle and were sitting behind a fallen tree where every shot or cry of pain could be heard clearly. "And there were some who yearned for a return to the better days. Many efforts were made to set us free but the citadel was too well guarded. Then the tyrant, fearful that the people would rise again under my father's leadership, had him removed by serving him a poisoned soufflé for dinner one evening. Shortly thereafter, the jailer, who had been an old family servant, managed to leave the dungeon door ajar and my two brothers and I escaped. My mother was too ill to travel and for all I know is still there.

"But that seems so long ago." She sighed again. "Soon after, we raised an army from the surrounding countryside and since that time have laid siege to the city. The battle has gone on year after year after year, and even though our cause is just we have never been able to gain the wall. It is always the same—charge and defeat, attack and retreat. My brothers fell in the early attacks as did almost all the men of our noble families. Only Ugolino, brave Count Ugolino, remains to lead us. But now he grows old and weary and each day there are fewer to follow. Our farms are stripped and bare, the land is black, and many of our soldiers are now just boys like yourself. But come, I will show you."

They moved still nearer, until they were at the very edge of the field, crouching behind the withered remains of some dead bushes. To their right a group of horsemen had reined up for a moment.

"How brave they are," he thought to himself, "and how few."

Just at that moment the city gate nearest them was flung open and from it galloped a heavily armed raiding party. They closed in quickly, surprising the young horsemen, and pressed their attack furiously. The skirmish dispersed in confusion across the dusty ground. Just in front of Claude and Elena a huge warrior singled out one of the boys and rode down on him hard, unseating him with one cruel thrust of his lance. Turning quickly, he reined in his horse, dismounted and unbuckled his mace. The boy looked up imploringly as the warrior stood over him, his armor gleaming.

"It is my cousin Nicolo," Elena cried.

Claude's breath came in short, sharp gasps and his heart pounded. Elena clutched his wrist, but just as the warrior raised the mace to strike he wrenched free, snatched up a heavy branch lying at his feet and leaped from behind the bush.

The startled soldier jumped back and lowered his weapon. Then in a moment his eyes narrowed and he spoke in a harsh and pitiless voice:

"Stand aside, stranger, or you too will die!"

Claude gripped the branch tightly. A small hard knot of

fear lodged in his chest, but he was determined and quick. Just as the warrior began to raise the mace again, he swung with all the force at his command. The branch struck the side of the warrior's head just below his helmet. He cried out in pain. Claude swung again, this time catching him on the joint of his right thumb, which caused him to drop the mace and howl again. The third blow landed just behind his left knee and he crumpled to the ground with a moan and a clatter. "Yield!" demanded Claude, pressing his knee to the hapless warrior's throat, and yield he did.

"How can we ever repay you?" Elena cried happily, but Claude was too happy to think of reward. Almost immediately a group of archers arrived to take the prisoner away and they all followed back to the encampment.

"You have performed a great service for us," said the aged Count Ugolino. "My days as a fighter are done, and as you can see, all does not go well. But today you have given us new hope. We cannot ask more of you."

"But you must let me help," Claude pleaded, for now there was something for which he knew he cared.

"It is far too dangerous," Elena insisted.

"And it is not even your cause," added the Count, but there was no way to dissuade him and by the time Claude left that afternoon he had vowed to fight until the city was theirs once more.

At first he helped only in those small ways where it was felt he could—tending the wounded, searching the countryside for food, patrolling the camp and repairing the weapons and armor. But soon that was not enough and he began to take part in the day's skirmishes, fearfully in the beginning, for now the flush of his first victory had faded, but still with great determination. From the rear of the battle line one day to the center the next and then finally to the front, he became in a very short time a seasoned soldier. Before long he had led his first assault on the wall, a

successful attack which set fire to one of the fortified towers, and soon after that he was leading them all.

Claude was everywhere indestructible—fighting, charging across the field with each attack, directing fire, encouraging the men, and pitting his strength and skill against the relentless enemy. From one grim battle to the next he grew stronger and more sure until his age and size no longer seemed to matter. His name became a rallying cry—*"Claudio! Claudio!"*—and a word that sent a shiver sliding into the boots of all those unfortunate enough to face him.

Day after day now, as soon as school had ended, weekdays and weekends too, he returned to the painting, fighting until the bell called him at six and then planning and waiting to begin again the next day.

Gradually the tide of battle began to shift. The army grew stronger and more confident under Claude's leadership and the siege grew more intense. An attack on the river gate, another on the west tower and a third on the arsenal—then a merciless bombardment of ballistas and mortars hurling fireballs of pitch and sulphur into the city and pounding the walls to pieces. Slowly the lines were drawn tighter and then tighter again as bowmen, crouching behind their barricades, swept the battlements clear. One afternoon, leading a picked group of men in a sudden rush, Claude actually held part of the wall for several hours, though almost at the cost of his life. And so it went, each new attack testing and probing and poking at the enemy's defenses until at last the time had come.

"I am convinced that we should attack at this point," he announced that afternoon. Everyone had gathered around to hear Claude outline his plan. The Count was there, with those still remaining from among the families exiled so long ago, and Elena, her eyes now bright with anticipation. Before them lay a map on which the sequence of battle was presented in great detail.

"The wall is strongest here," Claude continued, pointing to the one bastion they had never been able to approach, "and so it is here that they will least expect us. But it is also here that for weeks our sappers have been digging, and now the wall is undermined and gunpowder charges set at its base. Tomorrow we shall attack first at these locations," and the tip of his sword touched lightly at several points on the map. "We shall attack until their attention is diverted and their defenses spread thin. Then at my signal the powder will be ignited—and we shall charge for the last time." When he stopped not a word was spoken. It was so daring, and so simple, but would it work?

D.G. 65

The next day was bright and clear as indeed all the days had been. Everything awaited Claude's arrival. A cloud of smoke hung heavily over the beleaguered city and the air was stilled as if in expectation of the events to come. Pikes, lances and swords were sharpened and ready. Ladders, ropes and grappling irons were assembled. Bows were tightened, armor polished and the horses brushed and shining. Everything was checked and rechecked, and everything was ready.

At 2:00 the bombardment began, and this time it was far greater than anything the enemy had ever seen before. Destruction rained into the city from every side until it was difficult to imagine that there was anything or anyone left within. It continued steadily for about an hour and then, at 3:00, stopped.

A troop of cavalry under Nicolo's command began to circle the walls, feinting here and then there, drawing fire and keeping the enemy's defenses spread over the entire perimeter of the city. At 3:20 the attacks began, pressed forward as if each one were to be the only one. In and out they went, back and forth and around, leaving the defenders confused and exhausted. At 3:45 their work was done and all drew back. For a moment the smoke and dust cleared as Claude stepped forward to see. Except for the sound of his footsteps everything was quiet. Every eye was now on him. He paused for a moment and then raised his sword high over his head.

In an instant, a thunderous explosion shook the ground and a great section of the wall burst apart as if an enormous fist had smashed through it. Stones, mortar and men toppled over each other and when the debris settled, a large gap remained in the city's defenses. Towards it, every man and boy now charged.

"Death to the tyrant!"

"To victory!"

"For Elena!" they shouted as they rushed towards the opening. The defenders hurled themselves into the breach and both armies collided in battle. Claude led the main assault, slashing his way forward, while other groups scrambled up and over the mounds of stone to gain the walls with ladders, ropes and even their fingernails. Back and forth they swarmed like two huge beasts in a deadly embrace. Again and again Claude's arm rose and fell and again and again his shield rang against blows intent on cutting him down.

4:00 . . . 4:10 . . . 4:15 . . . 4:25 . . .

4:40. The battle raged on, with neither side gaining a foot nor giving an inch. Claude fought in a fury, forgetting all else, rallying his men and leading them time after time into the enemy line.

4:45 . . . 4:55 . . . 5:10 . . . 5:25 . . . 5:30 . . .

5:45, and still they fought—until at last the enemy began

to yield and draw back, exhausted and defeated. Claude waved his soldiers into the city and in they leaped. Then before doing so himself, he climbed to the top of the battered wall and looked out once more at all that he had fought for and wanted so much.

"Tomorrow it will be changed," he thought. "The city will be ours and Elena will always smile." Then just as he was about to shout "*Victory!*" himself and enter the city to claim it, the museum bell once more informed him of the time. That too would have to wait for tomorrow.

Claude didn't sleep at all that night. He tossed and

turned and paced, was up at seven, dressed at eight-thirty and out by nine-thirty. It was Saturday and the museum opened at ten, but he was at the doors by nine-twenty-five. They were closed and locked, of course. For a few minutes he fidgeted and waited in hopes that someone would let him in, then turned and raced down the steps and around to the side where he found the small door which had been left open for the guards and porters. He tiptoed along the dark service corridor and up the back stair to the main floor. Then, looking carefully to be sure that no one would stop him, he rushed across the floor to the alcove. There was the picture and Elena—but there also, on the floor directly below the painting, was a bucket and a mop with its handle resting against the frame. As he stood in the still-darkened corner, one of the porters walked past slowly and without looking to one side or the other reached down, picked them both up, and carried them away. There where the mop had stood was a small clear pool of liquid.

Claude was stunned. "They were not tears?" he asked softly, but there was no one to answer. What else was there to believe? "Was it only a dream?"

He looked at Elena's face, but now it seemed neither happy nor sad, and the river was only a ribbon of paint and surely no one had ever crossed that bridge, and the victory—what nonsense!

He sighed, and stood quietly for a moment. "But what does it matter?"

He turned and left the way he had entered, but had he stayed a few more minutes he might have seen the museum director, who had also arrived early that morning, summon the porter to him. And if he had been a little closer he might perhaps have heard him say how displeased he had been to see a mop resting against one of the paintings. And then also he would most probably have heard the porter apologize for not knowing better, for as he explained most reasonably, it was only his first day at the job.

But Claude had gone, and what has happened to him since is something we do not know. It is also hard to say for certain whether or not the events which took place really happened at all, for the one obscure chronicle which might have recorded them disappeared long ago in another and not dissimilar battle, and who else is there to tell us? Whether Claude ever returned to the museum is again a question about which we can only wonder, but it is still there, and if one day you should happen to be in the vicinity you must pay it a visit. Make it a point to see the Dutch collections and the English landscape painters and, of course, the Chinese

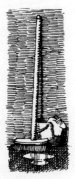

porcelains. And if you have a moment, stop and look at the "Young Lady in a Make-Believe Landscape," for she too is still there, in the alcove. Notice the beautiful modeling of her face, the careful balance of the composition, the great sense of space and depth in the background. Look also for the deftly controlled brushwork and the artist's great understanding of nature. But please—do not look for tears.

Good King RNP paced dejectedly in the throne room of his palace. That is, if you could call it a palace or for that matter even a throne room. In fact, there was also some confusion as to why he was called "Good," and beyond that the name RNP itself seemed to raise more questions than it answered. Nevertheless he paced, and as to his dejection there was no question at all, for RNP was the ruler of what was surely the most destitute and miserable kingdom in the world—that is, if you could call it a kingdom. It certainly didn't look like one.

The streets were a sea of mud, unpaved, rutted and very

difficult to use, except during the rainy season, when they were impossible to use. The buildings (those that were still standing) were in a state of complete disrepair—roofs leaked, floors sagged, doors jammed, and they hadn't been painted for so long that the original colors had faded past memory. The public fountain had long since run dry, the market shed had collapsed, and the stable roof had disappeared some time back, in a high wind. The weather was almost always too cold except when it was too hot, or too wet or too dry, and the poor farmers had a terrible time scratching a living from the barren, rocky soil. Melons would grow only to the size of grapefruits, grapefruits were no larger than oranges, the oranges were scarcely bigger than lemons, the lemons were merely the size of cherries, and the cherries were so small and bitter that everyone preferred to eat the melons.

As for RNP himself, things were no better. He was a small man with sad grey eyes and doubtful feet who wore hand-me-down clothes and a hand-me-down expression and no one paid any attention to him at all. For him there were no cheering crowds, no speeches, no victory parades, no medals to give, no babies to kiss, no foreign envoys with precious gifts—in short, nothing. In fact most people had forgotten who he was entirely, and because of his shabby appearance he was often asked to do odd jobs or run errands.

Even the dogs were impolite. So he spent most of his time at the palace.

But the palace was hardly more than a ruin. Its one main room served as the royal sitting room and bedchamber, kitchen and pantry, parlor, exchequer, banqueting hall, council chamber, gallery, grand ballroom, post office, and storeroom for the royal cabbages, which grew, of course, no larger than Brussels sprouts. All that distinguished it from the other buildings were the chipped and faded letters tacked up over the door which spelled out GOOD KING RNP. But why RNP? And then again, why Good? It is certainly about time that someone asked.

Many years ago, when the old king died, he had left his son as heir to the throne—a pale disinterested boy with no illusions. On the day of his coronation, when the royal storage chest was opened, it was discovered that along with the cast-iron crown and a somewhat moth-eaten robe, the only official letters left that had not been gnawed by the rats or ruined by the damp were an R, an N and a P. Since the kingdom was as poor then as it is now, there was no money available to buy others and so, after a hurried conference, the boy, who had been brought up to expect the worst, became RNP. (There was a strong sentiment for NRP, but a majority of citizens felt that it sounded a bit foreign.) The GOOD and the KING were added several years later when they were

found quite by accident at the bottom of the moat. From that time on, this is how it had been and as far as he knew this is how it would always be.

And so he paced and sighed, and sighed and paced. And on occasion, he would stop and gaze longingly at the distant mountains and wonder if somewhere in the world it was possible that there was something better, for he had no way of knowing that the same dry and dusty wind that stung his cheek would rise up afterwards into those mountains, freshen itself on the backs of the clouds—gently draw perfume from the tall pines and high grasses—throw off its cares, bouncing gaily from peak to valley to peak, and then drop softly to the broad green plain on the other side and lightly rustle the rich brocaded draperies in the palace of King Magnus the Abundant.

King Magnus sat contentedly in one of his nine royal dining rooms, eating breakfast. He nibbled daintily at each of the forty-three delicious courses prepared by the royal chefs and served with grace and elegance by the twenty-seven footmen and waiters carefully trained for just such employment. The bright morning sunlight streamed into the room, pausing only to acknowledge the leaded windowpanes before leaping joyfully from the gold and silver plates to the jeweled goblets, to the crystal chandelier, along the delicately carved moldings which lined the walls and ceiling, and finally spilling in great golden splashes onto the polished marble floor. Magnus smiled. If ever a king had reason to smile, he did. And then he laughed, and if he had reason to smile he surely had as much reason to laugh, for it would be hard to imagine a wealthier king or a richer and happier kingdom. From the palace itself if you were to look in any direction as far as the eye could see, and then from that distant point look again as far, and then look once more, you would only begin to understand the extent of this favored realm.

It was a land of bountiful orchards, fat farms, busy workshops and happy people, and in order to make certain that everything remained so, the seasons themselves seemed to be in competition to see which could be most splendid and helpful. The summers were warm and bright and busy. The autumns, amber and ample. The winters, crisp and sharp and full of steamy laughter, and the spring, shy and gay, smelling of recent rain. The roads were smooth and broad and they dipped and rose lazily with the easy rolling ground, curving gracefully back and forth through fields and woods as if reluctant to hurry through the lovely countryside before coming, finally, to the city itself.

And what can be said of the city? That the sun shining off its bright tile roofs made each street look like a necklace of precious jewels could be seen by anyone who had ever come down the road on a fine morning. That flowers hung at every window and that everything was freshly scrubbed and

 brightly painted and then scrubbed and painted again was obvious, surely, to everyone. That the streets were made of the finest cut stone, fitted with such skill that it was possible to run the length of any of them with a full glass of water and not spill a drop could be proved by anyone who had run the length of one with a full glass of water. That the palace contained eight hundred and twelve rooms, three thousand four hundred and fifty-eight windows, and forty-seven balconies was easily verified by anyone who cared to count, and that King Magnus at that very moment had just stepped out onto one of those balconies to greet his subjects was more than confirmed by the deafening shouts and cheers of the crowd below.

Magnus the Abundant was loved, as his father had been loved and his father before that and his father before that and back for a thousand years. Everywhere he went the crowds gathered to cheer him on his way or on his return, or to listen enthusiastically to a speech or a holiday oration. Banners were waved, songs sung, parades held, games staged, and always on everyone's lips was the name MAGNUS, MAGNUS, MAGNUS—or as many citizens of longer memory preferred, MAGNUS, MAXIMILIAN ALEXANDER (after his father), ROLAND, BENTIVOGLIO (after a distant relation who had distinguished himself in a long-forgotten war in a manner that no one could recall), HILARY, MANFRED, CHRISTOPHER, APOLLODORUS (the contribution of a maiden aunt who was fond of the classics), NICHOLAS, ADRIAN, FREDERICK, DIEGO ACOSTA Y RODRIQUEZ (after an uncle who had been lost once in Spain), AUGUSTUS, ALFRED, SEPTI-MUS (after a seventh cousin), BENEDICT CHARLES, GODFREY, LLEWELLYN, GILBERT, EDWARD, RALPH—which was, of course, his full name and could be shouted only during long parades or on afternoons which were not overly busy.

And so he stood on the balcony, as broad as his smile and as tall as his troubles were short. The ermine-trimmed cape he wore fell softly from his shoulders and the ruby and emerald crown sat on his head as lightly as only rubies and emeralds can. At his right hand was the beautiful Queen Goode and to his left, sturdy Prince Paragon and little Princess Ultima who, it was said, was so gentle and knowing that she could hear the flowers grow. Again and again he raised his arm and waved. "How happy," he thought, "how indescribably happy."

Meanwhile, though, many miles and many moods away, King RNP still paced in his one squalid room.

"How sad," he was heard to mumble, "how utterly sad."

"It could be much worse," answered a melancholy voice from the corner. It was Goom, the Prime Minister.

Now, while Magnus had scores of ministers, generals, admirals, ambassadors and servants, RNP had only Goom, who was the most miserable and pessimistic of all his subjects. His mother's name had been Gloom and his father's name Doom and since he was at least as unhappy as they were together, he was named for them both. Besides being Prime Minister he was also Foreign Secretary, Keeper of the Royal Seal, Minister of the Interior, Game Warden, Commander-in-chief of the Army and the Navy, Postmaster General and everything else, for each of which he was paid the same salary—nothing. It was also Goom's house which was the palace and so he lived there with the King, who, as was only proper, cooked and cleaned to earn his keep, and whenever RNP complained or grew too disconsolate Goom was there to cheer him up.

"It is never so dark that it can't get darker," he would grumble, or, "Whatever happens today is always better than what will happen tomorrow."

"There is no one who has as little as I," RNP would reply bitterly while clearing the dishes or mopping the floor, for it was this suspicion which made his unhappiness so much the sharper. "Somewhere there must be a king who has more!" And then Goom would again express his doubts, and as Minister of Finance go back to figuring how much money they didn't have in the treasury or as Royal Meteorologist return happily to predicting three weeks of continuous rain.

But today, in some mysterious way, it was different. A deep and irrepressible yearning had come over RNP. It had begun a long time ago as a small spot of uncertainty which drifted only occasionally into his thoughts, but now had grown and spread until he could think of nothing else. Back and forth and back and forth he paced with it, until suddenly he stopped and said in a soft voice, "I shall take a trip and see."

Goom looked up, and the surprise that appeared on his face was only matched by the dismay in his heart.

"I must find out what lies beyond those mountains," RNP continued, and Goom knew from the tone of his voice that he meant to do just that. No amount of argument could discourage him. Cries of "Nonsense!" and "Under no conditions!" were hardly even heard. Assurances of disaster or, at best, calamity couldn't change his mind. No guarantees that he would be "Eaten by bears!" "Waylaid by bandits!" "Drowned in a cataract!" or "Buried in an avalanche!" had any effect whatsoever, and the very next morning they left.

RNP had packed all his posses- sions in an old handkerchief and Goom, who was going along only to protect the King (since who knows how much worse the next king would be), brought little more than a frown. As Minister of  Transportation, though, he was able to find a small, rather smelly mule which naturally he rode while the King walked slowly behind. As they carefully picked their way along the muddy street, RNP paused to wave goodbye to the few uninterested citizens they passed.

"Farewell, loyal subjects, I shall return. Farewell, farewell." But as usual there was no response—except from a small boy who inquired softly, "Who's he?"

And so they traveled, under a grey and cheerless sky, and within a few hours their own poor kingdom had disappeared behind them. Only the mountains lay ahead. When they had finished their lunch of slightly stale bread and barely moldy cheese, RNP unfolded the old map he had found stuffed in a crack in the palace wall. He studied it carefully for many minutes, and when he finally made his decision and said "Here!" his finger was pointing almost exactly at the spot where Magnus the Abundant then stood.

Magnus too was thinking, and amidst all his happy and

contented thoughts was one which caused the slightest
shadow to cross his mind. "This should not be," he thought.
It was not fitting for him to have grave thoughts. Wasn't his
every wish instantly gratified? Wasn't there always something new and exciting to do? From early morning when two
valets drew his bath (one for the cold water and one for the
hot) till late in the evening when the court musicians finished their last lullaby, weren't all his needs taken care of immediately? Didn't his chamberlains and ministers and
generals assure him constantly that "Things couldn't be better," or that "One couldn't ask for more"? All this was true,

but hard as he tried to dismiss it from his thoughts, the doubt persisted—like a weed which, once rooted, can grow in the darkest, most inhospitable places.

"Perhaps somewhere there is someone else who has more than I," he thought, and this is what so disturbed his peace of mind. For as with many men who have much (and not only kings), it is only the thought of more which pleases them, or of having less than someone else which haunts their dreams. It was not a generous or a noble thought, yet there it was and there it had persisted for months, intruding on his otherwise perfect happiness. The Queen had noticed his somber mood and did her thoughtful best to cheer him up. The Prince and Princess sang only new songs and even the royal jesters made extra efforts, which did delight him—but not *quite* as much as they should have. No one knew what it was that bothered the King so. Even the royal physician, after a thorough examination, could find nothing wrong, but in order to be absolutely sure he prescribed several different kinds of pills and a change of scenery. "A fine idea," the King thought to himself. "I'll take a trip and see for myself."

"A marvelous idea," all the ministers agreed and each of them knew the perfect place to go.

74

"The Crystal Lagoon," suggested one, who was fond of fishing.

"The Faroff Valley," offered another, who had family in the vicinity.

"The Forest of Singing Birds," said a third, who knew of the King's fondness for music, and each in turn offered his choice.

But Magnus had other thoughts on his mind. "I have seen and enjoyed all that is in my kingdom," he said, "but what do I know of the world?" As he spoke his eye searched the enormous map which hung on the wall. In a few moments he stopped and touched the tip of his long pointer to one spot. "I shall visit here," he said. The ministers stared in horror, for the King had fixed his glance on that parched and unpromising land from which RNP and Goom had so recently departed, and they knew of course, as he didn't, what a poor and miserable place it was.

The prospect of the trip had restored the King's spirits and no one could persuade him to go elsewhere. Preparations were quickly made, and that very afternoon Magnus, the Queen, the Prince and the Princess in a golden carriage drawn by eight midnight-black horses with twenty-three supply wagons, seven cooks, five bakers, eleven valets, forty-three assorted servants, and an escort of the King's own royal guard departed with the heartfelt cheers and wishes of the entire population ringing in their ears.

Back at the palace, however, things were not nearly so gay. A gloomy gathering of the King's ministers sat worrying about the journey, for the King had never been beyond the borders of his own kingdom before and for all of his life had been shielded from everything but happiness and perfection. It was thought certain by all that the poverty and sorrow of

RNP's poor kingdom would surely make him sad again, and that if there were no cheers, no friendly crowds, no flowers, no flags, his poor heart must surely be broken.

"But what if there *are* cheers and crowds and flowers and flags," said one of the ministers suddenly, "and beautiful buildings with shiny brass knobs and paved roads too—and all the things the King has come to expect, and even some he's never seen."

"What indeed!" they all agreed, but how it was to be done was another matter.

"It will not be difficult at all," the minister continued, "for the royal party has taken that road which winds gently through the mountains. It is the easy and the long way around. If we"—and by this time the others were leaning forward in their seats—"if we take the short route, we can be there fully a week before the King and make preparations for his arrival—"

"Why of course!" they shouted. "How simple! Just what I was thinking," each admitted, and immediately plans were made and messengers dispatched throughout the countryside to inform the people. Because of their love for king and kingdom every man, woman, child, dog, cat and canary volunteered to help, and before the day had passed, the front end of a caravan that seemed to stretch from yesterday to next week had already begun to roll towards the mountains.

Down the royal road and out of the capital city they went, hundreds of wagons and carts packed with people and tools, pots of paint, buckets of nails, bags of mortar and numberless crates filled with the kinds of things that are always very useful if only you have them at the time you need them.

The royal architect had brought along his entire staff, plus pencils, erasers, T-squares, drawing boards, measuring tapes and blueprints for building everything from a palace to a bird bath. The carpenters had their saws and axes gleaming sharp. The masons, plasterers and painters itched to begin their work. The seamstresses were already sewing flags and bunting and the royal gardener was busy transporting every conceivable variety of tree and flowering bush as well as four wagons full of rich manure. It took hours for the gay and noisy caravan to pass, but before long all that remained was a cloud of dust and the echo of their many gay songs. A strange silence settled over Magnus's kingdom, for everyone—everyone— had gone.

Unaware of what was happening on the other side of the mountains, RNP and Goom, riding and walking by turns, continued slowly along their unhappy way across the steep and rocky trails. To Goom's surprise, the trip was proceeding much better than expected. It was true, of course, that it had rained almost continuously and that they had taken several wrong turns and that they had forgotten to bring matches or

blankets or clean socks, but they had only *almost* been drowned in a cataract and not completely buried in an avalanche, and the one time that they were waylaid by bandits, the startled outlaws had been so moved by RNP's plight that they gave him everything they owned.

Magnus, though, was enjoying himself immensely. On his side of the mountain the sun shone continuously with only an occasional soft breeze to interrupt its steady warmth, almost as a reminder of how good it felt. The great golden coach glided easily along the broad country road and the days were filled with picnics and song, armfuls of flowers, large juicy apples and afternoon naps in the high meadows. As they drew ever nearer to RNP's kingdom, the happy King, save for his one distant doubt, could hardly conceive of a happiness to equal his.

And so they traveled—Magnus and RNP—RNP and Magnus—one seeking more happiness and the other, less misery.

Meanwhile, hurrying by day and by night without stop or rest, the eager caravan arrived finally at the wretched and joyless state which RNP called home. With no time to spare, everything was quickly unloaded and work begun. "Quick, bring the ladder here!"—"Nails, more nails!"—"Out of the way! Out of the way!"—"Pick it up!"—"Put it there!"—"Let it go!"—"Put it down!"—"Paint it purple!"

Instructions and orders, shouts and suggestions mingled in the air with the clangs, clashes, buzzes and bumps of work being done,  and even the local citizens, who understood little and cared less, paused to watch as the city was transformed before their eyes. All the buildings were carefully repaired and painted, windows replaced, delicately carved cornices and pediments added where appropriate, steps rebuilt, and all hinges, locks, knobs, handles and hooks polished until the brasswork shone like precious metal. The streets were leveled and paved and a line of decorative linden trees was planted from the new palace to the edge of the city. Charming flowerbeds in intricate geometric patterns were planted in the public gardens and the bright flags which were flown from every top and tower slapped at the wind as if to announce, "Look, we're new!" Everything that could be moved was repaired and everything else was scrubbed, and in seven days and nights the job was done, the tools put away, the wagons hidden and the waiting begun. One lone sentry was posted in the tallest tree to signal the King's coming and as a final touch garlands of flowers were strung throughout the night.

The very next morning, King Magnus's carriage appeared in the distance, and as the sentry's signal sounded, eager and anxious faces filled the streets. As he drew closer and closer the excitement mounted. The busy ministers, staying carefully out of sight, bustled about giving instructions and as the golden coach entered the city a wave of cheers and shouts swept forward to meet it—and then another and another and again and again until the waves became an ocean which seemed to engulf the King. The band struck up an inspiring medley of marches as the crowd strained forward, and up ahead scores of children carpeted the ground with rose petals. Slowly and majestically the coach moved forward as the King acknowledged the joyful crowds.

"What a beautiful city this is!" said the Queen. "The people are so friendly it's almost as if we knew them." The King continued to smile and wave, and the crowd to cheer. On they drove, past the palace, which had been entirely rebuilt of beautiful salmon-colored brick, and the public square with its new marble fountain sending delicate streams of water into the air.

"One certainly could ask for no more," said the Prince, who was more than pleased with everything. At that the King seemed to smile a little less and grew thoughtful.

Up the avenue and under the eaves of the brightly painted houses and shops they continued. Geraniums, petunias and violets tumbled over each other from every windowbox and fine merchandise was tastefully displayed in all the shop windows.

"It really couldn't be better," cried the delighted Princess, turning round and round so as not to miss anything. And now the King stopped smiling entirely.

"What a fortunate man must rule in this beautiful country," everyone agreed, and as they reached the far end of the city with the shouts and happy cries still echoing, a frown appeared on Magnus's face—for what must have been the first time in his life. The seed of that one small doubt he had carried with him for so long had now blossomed into a flower of discontent. His suspicions, it seemed, had all been true.

"Everyone has as much as I," he thought unhappily, "and who knows how many have more?"

All his happiness was gone, for the long journey had only proved what he feared most. And so he ordered the carriage to turn down the road towards the mountains, and without a word or a smile they headed for home.

But no cheers and no crowds greeted RNP when after many, many days of difficult travel he and Goom finally crossed over into Magnus's kingdom. By this time their clothes were even more ragged than when they had set out and the poor mule was hardly able to complete the last stages of the trip. In the distance lay the city, the magnificent city

that Magnus had left. But there had been changes here too. In one of those unexplainable turns that nature sometimes takes, a great storm, the first for many years, had ripped and raged across the countryside. Whether or not it was the result of vagrant winds or an unfortunate conjunction of the stars or simply the weather's angry reply to those who had left this favored valley untended cannot be said, but trees had been uprooted and scattered about, roofs carried off, windows broken, houses hurled to the ground or sorely battered and everything covered with layers of mud and debris—and now no one was there to set it right. It seemed a much different city when RNP and Goom came at last to the outskirts. The last heavy grey clouds of the storm still hung overhead and the muddy and empty streets were strewn with bits and pieces of trees and buildings. Many of the shutters and doors hung crazily by one hinge or else had dropped off altogether and all the flags and banners and flowers were gone. "Just as I suspected," Goom grumbled, for it fulfilled all his melancholy expectations. And the King, now hunched sadly on the little mule, rode on into the deserted city. The squish of their footsteps echoed strangely in the quiet and all around the windows frowned down on them.

"It is far worse than your own kingdom," continued Goom as they passed the silent palace, stepping carefully over several fallen trees. The south wing had been caved in by a toppled oak and several of the turrets and a balustrade had simply disappeared, giving it all a sad and ruined look. The slightest smile unexpectedly tugged at the corners of RNP's mouth.

"No one has even come out to bid you welcome," Goom went on as they turned into the now dismal public square (he wished merely to point out to RNP the folly of his ways). The shops, which had been boarded up when everyone had gone, remained so, and the market stalls were now strewn about everywhere. And the King now smiled a broad and happy smile. Then as they reached the far end of the city and the row of mud-spattered and dingy houses gave way to flattened fields, he laughed, for perhaps the first time that anyone could remember.

"I was wrong," he cried happily, as he brushed the mud from his ragged cloak. "See for yourself, no king lives better than I. I have as much as anyone." And even though nothing had changed he felt as if a weight had been lifted from his heart.

Suddenly the grey and overcast day was just perfect, the future bright, and even his thoroughly disreputable appearance the height of fashion.

"Come, come, Goom!" he shouted impatiently. "It's time we were returning to our own beautiful kingdom."

With a wave of his tarnished crown and a last look at the

exquisite desolation he was leaving behind him, RNP turned the puzzled mule in the direction from which they'd come. And as he galloped down the road, poor Goom, who was doing his best to keep up (for it is difficult to complain and run both at the same time), fell further and further behind.

So the two kings traveled towards home and this is where we must leave them, for what they found on their return and how they lived their lives from then on is, of course, another story. To Magnus everything now seemed like nothing, and to RNP nothing had become quite enough. One was happy and the other sad, and perhaps it is not unreasonable to expect that on the long, arduous ride back, each of them might have wondered why.